THE WAR WITH GRANDPA

by

Robert Kimmel Smith

illustrated by Richard Lauter

A YEARLING BOOK

Published by
Bantam Doubleday Dell Books for Young Readers
a division of
Bantam Doubleday Dell Publishing Group, Inc.
1540 Broadway
New York, New York 10036

ISBN: 0-440-49276-9

Reprinted by arrangement with Delacorte Press

Printed in the United States of America

October 1984

46   45   44   43   42   41

OPM

For Grandpa Teddy

CONTENTS

Contents

THE WAR WITH GRANDPA

1

PETER STOKES'S TRUE AND REAL STORY

This is the true and real story of what happened when Grandpa came to live with us and took my room and how I went to war with him and him with me and what happened after that.

I am typing it out on paper without lines on my dad's typewriter because Mrs. Klein, she's my 5th grade English teacher, said that we should write a story about something important that happened to us and to tell it "true and real" and put in words that people said if we can remember and to put quote marks around them and everything.

She also said to keep the sentences short. Looking back on how I began, I can see I'm doing terrible already. The first two sentences took up almost ½ the page.

My little sister, Jennifer, just came in and asked me what I'm doing and I told her. She told me to put Pac-Man in my story and maybe Wonder Woman she watches reruns of every afternoon on Channel 6. "No," I said.

"Why not?"

"Because it is a story about Grandpa and me, silly. Not some made-up thing like on TV."

"Could it have a horse in it?" she asked.

Jennifer loves horses a lot. She cuts pictures of them out of magazines and tacks them up on the wall in her room. "No horses."

"A magic fairy?"

"No!"

"I bet it's going to be a stupid story," she said.

Jennifer was wearing a Pac-Man cap, her Superman T-shirt, a jeans belt that said JEANS on it, and sneakers that said LEFT and RIGHT on the toes. She looked like a walking billboard.

"It is going to be a great story," I said.

"How does it begin?"

"I don't know. That's what I was trying to remember when you came marching in."

"I think it should begin with me," Jenny said, "because I found out Grandpa was coming to live here before you even knew about it."

"Good idea," I said.

"And put in the story that I am very beautiful with long blond hair and lovely blue eyes."

"I just did."

"Now you'll have a good story," she said.

2

THE BEGINNING

I like to read stories that have lots of chapters that are short. Because it makes the book go faster and you always can find your place. So you can bet my story is going to have a bunch of teeny-tiny chapters.

It really began when Jennifer came into my room with that look on her face that usually means she knows something that I don't. That's one thing Jennifer likes best in life—a secret. Not that she is so good at keeping secrets. She is no good at all in that department. In fact, I can usually get her to tell me anything I want because I'm her big brother and she's only a little kid.

"I know something you don't," Jennifer said. She headed across my room to the broken rocking chair.

"Don't sit on my rocker," I replied.

She looked at me and made one of her faces

where her eyes roll back in her head and she pouts. "Why not?"

"Because you will make the arm pop out of the back like you always do because you rock too hard."

"I will not," she said, which was a lie. She always breaks my rocker.

The rocker used to be in the living room until it broke. My mom was going to throw it in the trash, but I rescued it and brought it up to my room. One of these days my dad says he will glue the arm really solid so it won't pop out all the time.

Jennifer was standing right near my rocker. "Don't even touch it!" I said before she could.

"Don't you want to know what I know?" Jennifer asked me.

"I already know everything you know and a whole lot more," I said. I picked up the book on my bed like I didn't want to talk anymore and pretended to begin reading.

"It's about Grandpa."

I kept on reading.

"Grandpa Jack."

I ignored her.

"From Florida."

That made me laugh. We have only one Grandpa Jack and he lives in Fort Lauderdale in Florida. "I remember him," I said.

"It's not funny, Peter Stokes," Jennifer said. "Grandpa Jack is too lonely down in Florida since Grandma died, so he sold their house and he's coming to live with us. Right here, in this very house. I heard Mom talking to Dad about it on the telephone. We're supposed to cheer him up, you and me, because his leg is hurting him a lot and all. And he's very sad about Grandma."

"Grandpa's coming to live here?" I said.

"Yop." She nodded.

"I'm glad," I said, and I was. I like Grandpa a lot, but I don't get to see him much because he lives so far away. "For once you found out a good secret, Jenny," I said.

"That's not the secret," she said, putting her hand on her hip and posing like a statue or something. "Where do you think his room will be?"

"I don't know. Upstairs on the third floor, probably, in the guest room."

She smiled and put her tongue between her teeth so it showed. "Oh, no," she said, "that's where you are going."

"Me!"

"Yop." She smiled at me because I was groaning out loud.

"You mean Grandpa is getting *my* room?"

"I can't tell you," Jennifer said. "That's the secret."

3

A ROOM
WITHOUT GLOOM

Let me tell you about my room. I love it!!!

I was born here. Well, I was born in a hospital, really, but I have lived in this room all my life. Ten years so far. My crib used to be in the corner near the window that looks out on the driveway. Now my bed is on the long wall. I have these bookshelves right behind my headboard and my high-intensity lamp is there too. My desk is in the corner where my crib used to be and I can look out the window while I do my homework. I have these yellow toy cabinets with all my stuff in them. On top of the cabinets are shoeboxes where I have all my baseball cards. There's a thick carpet on the floor that used to tickle my feet when I was little. And I have a poster up on the wall over my dresser of Hank Aaron hitting his 715th home run.

This room is MINE. Nobody else in my family ever lived here. Nobody. I know how my room is in the morning, when the sun peeps over the roof of the Murphy house behind ours and comes through my venetian blinds. I know the sound when it rains hard and pings against the windows and the drainpipe outside. I can get up out of my bed in the middle of the night and walk around my room without even looking because I know where every single thing is.

Nothing about my room is scary. When floorboards creak at night I know it's floorboards and not some monster. When the wind rubs the maple tree against the side of the porch outside I'm not afraid some crook is sneaking into our house.

When you live in a room your whole life, that room is yours. It doesn't belong to Jennifer, or my mom or my dad. And it certainly doesn't belong to Grandpa Jack, who never even lived one day in this house.

This room is mine. I love it. I belong in it. And I don't ever want to live anywhere else.

4

THE DEADLY DINNER

This chapter is about what happened at dinner that night. I'm not too proud about how I acted, but I'm going to write it anyway. Because it is true and real.

I didn't go dashing off to my mother when Jennifer dropped the news on me about Grandpa coming. I have a feeling about bad news. I always let it come to me instead of running around like an idiot looking for it.

But I can tell you I was feeling pretty awful that whole afternoon. And I didn't have much appetite for dinner.

My dad came home at his usual time that night, about six o'clock. My dad's name is Arthur and he's an accountant. An accountant works with money, in case you didn't know, figuring out how much money people and companies have and what they should do with money besides spending it. In the spring when people have to pay their income taxes my dad is very busy and sometimes comes home very late and even works on weekends. Tax Time, he calls it, and it goes on for months. During Tax Time he disappears downstairs into his office in the basement and doesn't come out until it's over.

Now, after telling you all that, I have to be truthful and say I don't know what Dad does *exactly*. Except he uses a calculator and some big books called ledgers a lot.

Anyway, we were on dessert and milk when the subject of Grandpa came up and it was Mom who spoke about it.

"Children," she said, "I have some wonderful news."

Wonderful? I was thinking. If this was wonderful then maybe Thursday was Sunday.

"You know that Grandpa Jack has been very sad down in Florida since Grandma died. Well, I was speaking to him the other day and guess what? He's sold the house down there and he's coming to live with us. Isn't that exciting?"

Mom was looking at me with such a happy expression on her face that I had to smile. Just a little. "Terrific," I said, which was maybe one of the biggest lies of my life.

"You'll finally get to know your grandpa,"

Dad said. "He's a great guy, Peter, and he loves you and Jenny a lot."

"I love him up to the sky and down to the ocean," Jenny said. "He always sends me candy on my birthday."

That's my silly sister. If Frankenstein gave her chocolate, she'd be his best friend.

"When is Grandpa coming?" I asked.

"In about a week," Mom said. "He's just finishing some last-minute things and then he'll fly up here to stay."

"We've got to make Grandpa feel welcome, kids," Dad said. "Our home is his home now. I expect you to treat him just like a member of the family. With respect and courtesy. And maybe with a little extra understanding because he misses Grandma so."

"It may be strange in the beginning," Mom said, "having Grandpa here all the time, but I know you'll do everything you can to make him happy."

"Can I show him my ballet routines?" Jenny asked.

"Perhaps," Dad said, smiling. "He'll probably enjoy them."

"Will he play the piano for me while I dance?"

"Not unless he's suddenly learned how to play the piano," Mom said.

"Will he play casino with me?" Jenny asked.

"Jenny," Dad said, "let's not jump all over Grandpa Jack the minute he walks in here. Let him settle in and get comfortable." Dad looked over at me. "Peter? Why so silent?"

"Just thinking," I said.

"Are you worried about Grandpa coming here?" Mom asked.

"A little," I said. I saw a funny look pass from Mom to Dad. "Where is he going to stay?" I asked. "In the guest room?"

"Well," Dad said with a kind of sigh, "no, Peter."

"Where then?" I asked. *"Exactly."*

"Let's talk about it," Dad began. "You see, Peter, Grandpa's leg is really bad. He can't walk stairs very well. So putting him on the top floor of the house, up two whole flights of stairs, that's not a good idea."

"And the bathroom on the top floor is only half a bath, Peter," Mom said. "If we put Grandpa up there, he'd have to go down a flight of stairs to shower, then up again."

"Couldn't you put a shower in the top-floor bathroom?" I asked.

"Not really," Dad said.

"Why not?" I said. "There's only those old dinky rooms up there where we store things away. You could make the bathroom bigger."

"Look, Peter," Dad said, "we've been thinking awfully hard about where Grandpa can stay, and there seems to be only one answer."

"*No!*" I said as fast as I could.

"It has to be your room, Peter," Dad said.

"Absolutely, positively, one hundred percent *no!* Spelled N-O!" I didn't just say that. I yelled it.

"Peter," Mom said, "don't shout."

"Don't you want Grandpa to live with us?" Jenny said. "How can you be so mean?"

"Stay out of this, birdbrain," I said to her.

"Oh, Peter." Dad sighed, shaking his head slowly.

"Why can't Jenny give up *her* room?" I asked. "Why does it have to be me?"

"She's still a baby, Peter," Mom said.

"I am not!" Jenny said. She looked insulted.

"She still gets up in the night sometimes," Mom went on. "And she needs looking after more than you do. Especially getting dressed in the morning. You know what a slowpoke she is, and how I have to keep after her or she'd be late for school every day. You're a big boy now, Peter, almost grown up. I depend on you; you know that."

"It's not fair," I said.

"It's not fair that Grandma died," Dad said. "It's not fair that Grandpa is so sad and lonely. Life isn't always fair, Pete."

"We'll try to make you as comfortable as possible on the third floor," Mom said. "Who knows? Maybe you'll enjoy living up there."

"Oh, no, I won't!" I cried out. "I love my room. It's mine!" And even as I said that, I knew it wouldn't do any good. So I did the only thing I could. I jumped up from my chair, ran up to my room, threw myself on the bed, and cried like a maniac.

5

SAD AND BLUE
AS THE SKY

Well, that is about as long a chapter as I ever care to write. It took about five days! I don't know how authors ever write big fat books. They must spend their whole life doing it.

Meanwhile, I was as sad as I ever was, up in my room, and about as blue as the sky.

There's a thing that happens when parents want kids to do something and the kid doesn't want to. What happens is that the parents usually win. That's one of the big advantages of being a parent. You get to win the arguments.

Take piano lessons, for example. Once a week I go to Mrs. Biddle's house and spend forty-five minutes plonking away at these stupid pieces while she sits beside me sighing and shaking her head. Do I want to take piano lessons? No. Do I have to? Yes. Do I want to practice the piano every afternoon after school? No. Does my mom make me do it? You know the answer.

Why couldn't I have baseball lessons instead?

If somebody pitched me a baseball for forty-five minutes every week, then maybe I could learn to hit a ball instead of striking out all the time. Which is what I do, except a few times by accident I hit the ball. Last year I got only two hits all season.

Anyway, what happened was that after a while my dad came up to my room and talked to me. I had that sinking feeling in my stomach the whole time we talked. I knew I was going to lose the argument. They couldn't move Jenny upstairs because she was still a baby, no matter what she says. And because Grandpa had a bad leg, he couldn't live on the top floor of our house. "I'm sorry, Pete, that's just the way it is," Dad said.

"Can I say I think it stinks?" I asked.

"Sure."

"It stinks."

"I agree with you," Dad said.

"It's disgusting, terrible, gross, and also horrible," I said.

"It sure is," Dad said. "We'll start moving some of your things upstairs this weekend. I'm sure you'll be comfortable up there."

"I'll hate it."

"If you have that attitude, you will hate it," Dad said. "Give it a chance, Peter."

"Do I have a choice?" I asked.

"No."

"Then I don't want to talk about it any-more."

And we didn't.

6

I PROMISE

I am putting down this promise in black and white so I don't ever forget it.

When I grow up and have a kid I will never make him do anything he really does not want to.

That is a solemn promise, so help me God.

Except if it is something really important. Like if he didn't want to brush his teeth, I'd have to make him do it or else he would get cavities and stuff.

Or if he didn't want to eat vegetables, say, and he would not get his vitamins to help him grow up right.

Or if he wanted to run across the street when a car was coming. I would have to stop that, of course.

Or if he fooled around with matches or electricity or poison or things that could hurt him.

And if he did not want to go to school, why,

20

I guess I'd have to make him go or he'd grow up stupid.

Maybe there's a few other things he'd have to do I have not thought of. But other than that, no.

And that's a promise.

7

BITS AND PIECES

I noticed that my sentences are getting too long again. I will write them shorter.

About my dad. He started moving things. My things. From my room. Up to the guest room. On the top floor. Which is also the third floor.

My toy cabinets. They are yellow Formica. With white tops. Two doors outside. Three shelves inside. And all my good stuff was in them. All my board games. Monopoly. Stratomatic Baseball. Clue. Careers. Risk. Snakes and Ladders. All my crayons in a plastic box. Most of them were broken anyway. Old coloring books I use only when I am home sick. All my baseball cards were on top of the cabinets in these shoeboxes. I have been saving them since I was seven. I have almost two thousand baseball cards. Counting extras.

Then my mom moved my summer clothes

upstairs. Into the closet in the guest room. My new room.

I had to help my dad move my bookcase upstairs. First I moved my trophies. They go on top of the bookcase. I had six of them. All gold. They were baseball trophies. From playing on my Beverly Boys' Club teams. Since I was six years old. Every kid who plays gets one. The other trophy was for a bowling tournament. I bowled a 96. My best score of all time.

Let me be honest. Every kid in the bowling tournament got one too.

To move the bookcase upstairs we first had to empty it. We put all my books on the floor first. All my Encyclopedia Brown books. All my Great Brain books. My whole collection of sports stories. All my paperbacks with baseball team records.

My room began to look empty when we got it all upstairs.

Then we moved my pictures from the walls. And hung them upstairs. Hank Aaron hitting his 715th home run. Tom Seaver pitching. The first astronauts on the moon. Some of my best drawings I made for school. Pretty soon my walls were naked.

Now my room looked weird. It didn't look

like my room anymore. Lying on my bed, I began to think it wasn't my room. Like I didn't belong there.

A few days before Grandpa came we moved my dresser. First we took the drawers out. Then we carried them upstairs one by one. Then we moved the dresser. It wasn't too heavy.

Then we moved the old dresser from the guest room down into my room. Every night I had to go upstairs to bring down my clean clothes for the next day.

We moved my desk next. It went upstairs into the corner of the guest room. I had to go up to the top floor every day after school to do my homework.

The only thing left in my room was my bed. And the night before Grandpa came we moved it upstairs too.

Now all the guest room stuff was in my room. And all my things were up on the top floor in the guest room.

"I guess you'll start sleeping up here tonight," my dad said.

I didn't say anything.

"Are you okay, Pete?" my dad asked. "You look like you're going to cry any second."

"I won't cry," I said. I hoped that was true.

"You'll get used to it," Dad said. He looked out of the window. "Nice view from up here. Take a look, Pete."

I stood next to my father and looked out. The Taub house was across the street. The streetlight on the corner showed through the trees. The tree on our lawn looked so close, I felt I could almost touch one of the branches.

My dad put his arm around my shoulders. "Growing up, Pete," he said, "it isn't easy. Sometimes you have to do things you don't like."

"I hate it up here," I said.

Dad sighed. "I know. But, Peter, you mustn't ever let Grandpa Jack know that. Or else he'll feel terrible. And believe me, he feels terrible already."

I didn't say anything when Dad hugged me. I didn't even feel any better either.

The last thing that was moved into the guest room was me.

8

NIGHT FRIGHT

I'm a little ashamed of this part of my story, but I have to tell the truth. Not only was I mad as a wet hairnet about losing my great room, I was a little bit scared about sleeping upstairs too.

I brushed my teeth and did my go-to-bed things in the top floor bathroom. Instead of the beautiful bathroom Jenny and I shared downstairs I had this dinky dim bathroom now. It was gross. The mirror was very old and had dark stains on it. The sink was very tiny and kind of yellow instead of being white. And the walls were dark old wood, like some rough cabin in the woods.

I went downstairs to my parents' bedroom and kissed Mom good night. On the way back upstairs I peeked into my old room. It looked strange to see different furniture in there. Strange and kind of hurting.

It was scary to go upstairs to my room. The

staircase leading to the top floor was narrow and rickety. The steps were bare wood that creaked when you stepped on them. And there wasn't too much light. Not like the steps leading to the second floor, which were covered with thick carpet and had a beautiful light fixture so everything was plain as day.

The hallway upstairs was spooky. A narrow little space that was very dark. With open doors to empty rooms that looked like black caves where someone could be hiding.

I know that sounds silly, but that's what I was feeling. There is no boogeyman who waits in the dark to grab kids. I know that. But at nine o'clock at night in this dim little hallway with the floorboards creaking you can get frightened whether you know that or not.

I kind of jumped into my new room and slammed the door shut fast. And just as fast jumped into bed and under the covers.

I waited awhile before I turned off my lamp. I was in no hurry for it to get dark. But finally I did it. And that turned out to be scary too.

Like I said before, in my old room I knew where everything was and how everything was and there was nothing scary. But up here it was different.

A light flickered on the ceiling and the wall,
making shadows that jumped around. And a rustling noise came from outside the window. And
something in the hallway made a sound. Was it
a footstep outside my door?

I may sound very brave just writing these
things down so easy. The truth was I was terrified
out of my mind. The waving shadows of yellow
light on the wall almost began to look like two
black arms that could grab me. "Be still my
heart," I whispered to myself. Which is something my mom says sometimes. I felt like an idiot
talking to myself, but I was the only company
I had in that room. "It's nothing," I said. I
crossed my fingers. Then I crossed my toes. Go
to sleep, I told myself. Just close your eyes and
fall asleep and everything will be hunky-dory.

Ha.

I got into my best sleeping position. Which
is curled up on my right side with my hands
tucked up under my cheek. The rustling sound
had to be from the big old tree outside my window, I figured after a while. And the spooky
yellow light was probably the streetlamp on the
corner. And the noises outside my door were
just old floorboards creaking. And there really

wasn't a crook or a murderer sneaking up here to get me.

Probably.

And then I began to get angry.

Why was I the only one in the house who had to give up something for Grandpa? Why me? And why was I stuck up here in this disgusting and scary place instead of staying in my great and wonderful old room?

I thought about my illustrated book of old sea battles and the picture of John Paul Jones on deck with his big curved sword in the air. "I have just begun to fight!" he said.

It gave me an idea. Maybe there was a way I could fight to get back what was really mine. But how?

That's what I was thinking about when I finally fell asleep.

9

GRANDPA JACK

Now I have to tell you about my grandpa Jack and what happened when he finally came to our house to live and how he settled in and everything like that.

And that's another too long sentence.

I used to know my grandparents very well when I was little and they lived close by. I remember they used to come to our house most weekends and they played with me a lot. But then Grandma got this terrible disease. They call it M-fazeema, but they spell it emphysema. It comes from smoking cigarettes, which if anybody does, they have to be crazy. This emphysema made it very hard for Grandma to breathe. Mom said that on windy or cold days Grandma was not allowed to put a foot outside her house. Or any other part of her either.

It was around then that Jenny was born. And Grandma and Grandpa moved to Florida.

Mom said it was for the warm weather, which was good for Grandma's lungs. I remember being sad when they left. I loved them a lot. I loved how they always wanted to play with me and almost anything I did was okay with them.

Starting then, I saw them only when we would go to their house in Florida at Christmas. The rest of the year we would talk on the telephone maybe once a week.

And then Grandma died.

Now Grandpa was alone and it was hard to think about. I only knew my grandma and grandpa together. They were never apart when they saw me and the family. They were a pair, like shoes or gloves. But now there was only Grandpa.

Dad brought Grandpa home from the airport. He pulled the car up in the driveway and tooted the horn. We all ran outside and Jenny jumped right on Grandpa's neck as soon as he got out of the car, even though Mom had just said not to. Dad finally had to take her down. Then Grandpa gave me a long hug and held me away to look at me. "You're no Peapod anymore," he said, which was a nickname he had called me. "Petey, you're springing up like a weed. You must have grown three inches since

Christmas!" He smiled at me then, with little lines crinkling up around his eyes. I smiled back at him.

He looked different to me from the last time I'd seen him. The lines and wrinkles in his tan face looked deeper. His shoulders stooped down, and there was kind of a sad look in his eyes even when he was smiling. And when we finally got into the house, with Dad and me helping to carry Grandpa's things, I could see that Grandpa was limping worse than ever.

Grandpa used to be in the construction business until he retired. Building houses, mostly. Years ago a big piece of wood fell on him and broke his leg. Mom and Grandma always said it never healed right. And now Grandpa had something wrong with his leg that Mom called arthritis.

It was late when Grandpa arrived and we all carried his things upstairs and tried to help him get settled into his room. My room, I mean, my old room that was now his. My idea of helpful was to take Grandpa's shirts out of his suitcase and put them into his dresser. Jenny's idea of helpful was to do pirouettes in the middle of the room, banging into everybody.

Mom finally shooed Jenny and me out and

made us get ready for bed. I did all my go-to-bed things and got into my pajamas and went downstairs to the kitchen to say good night to Mom and Dad. They were sitting at the kitchen table, drinking tea. I knew when I walked in that they were saying private things to each other because they shut up quick when I came in and looked at me kinda funny. My mom looked real sad, like she was getting ready to cry. She hugged me a little extra tight, I thought, and ruffled my hair. I said good night.

I didn't go back to my room though. What I did was hang around under the staircase to hear what they were saying. I was right about my mom; she was crying. "He looks so awful," she sobbed.

"Please, Sally," I heard my dad say. "He's very tired, you know. It's been a very long day for him. He'll be fine after he gets some rest."

"There's just no life in him," Mom said. "No life."

"It's only a few months since she died," Dad said. "He's very depressed. Give it time, hon."

"I hope you're right," Mom said.

I sneaked up the stairs very quietly, so my folks couldn't hear me, and went to say good night to Grandpa. He was sitting on the edge of the bed, holding something in his hand. I could see it was a photograph of Grandma in a silver frame. "Good night, Grandpa," I said, but I don't think he heard me. He just kept very still, staring at Grandma's face in the picture.

My mom was right, I thought as I went up to my room. Grandpa had no life at all. Could you die from being sad? I wondered. Could you?

10

ANOTHER NIGHT, ANOTHER FRIGHT

It was still scary upstairs in my new room. Maybe even more than it was the night before.

The floorboards creaked again. The same shadows and light danced around on the ceiling. I still had the thought that a murderer was waiting outside my door to come in and kill me in my bed.

You can laugh all you want. I was scared silly.

11

ONLY A DOPE
WILL MOPE

Now I have to tell you about a special word. It's called *mope*.

My sister Jenny does that a lot. She's a real moper, Mom says. It means standing around with your face hanging out and looking like doomsday is tomorrow. "Only a dope will mope," Mom says to Jenny all the time. Usually Jenny mopes when she wants Mom to stop what she's doing and play cards with her, or something. Naturally, Jenny always does her moping when Mom is real busy. Like before dinner or lunch, or when Mom is about to go shopping or clean up something. "Not now," Mom says, "and don't mope."

The reason I'm telling you about moping is because that is exactly what Grandpa was doing. Except he called it resting. He hung around in his room practically all the time. When I asked him to take a walk somewhere with me he'd just say: "No, thanks, Petey, I'll just rest here awhile." Sometimes he'd do his sitting in the living room. And that's all he'd do, sit. He'd sort of stare into the air, not even pick up a magazine or watch TV.

Or after lunch sometimes I'd ask him to have a catch with me, or maybe walk down to the candy store and get an ice cream cone. "Not today, Petey, thanks," he'd say. And he'd sit on the porch or in the living room and just do nothing.

I'll bet in the first couple of weeks he was living with us he never even went as far as around the corner. He just sat around. That wasn't how he acted before he went to Florida and Grandma died. Back then, when I was little, I remember how peppy he was.

"We'll have more fun than a barrel of monkeys," Grandpa used to say. And we did. He used to take me places like the park and the zoo. I was always happy when I was with him. I liked everything about him. His little white moustache that jumped up and down when he talked. The way he'd throw me up in the air and catch me, or spin around fast, holding me in his arms. Even his breath, which always smelled of peppermints.

I liked the way he'd toss me a ball and I'd try to catch it. I was little then and could hardly hold on to the ball, but it was fun playing with him.

I know Mom and Dad were concerned about Grandpa and the way he just seemed to be tired out and moping all the time. We went out to the movies a couple of times, and to a restaurant, but Grandpa always stayed home. "You go ahead," he'd say, "I'll be okay back here by my lonesome."

"Come on," Dad would say, "we'll have some fun."

"Have fun then," Grandpa would say. "I'd only spoil it for you."

I saw the worried looks that passed between Mom and Dad. But when I asked Dad about it he just said, "Grandpa's a little tired, Peter, that's all. He'll snap out of it soon."

Sure, I thought, but how soon was soon?

12

A LITTLE HELP
FROM MY FRIENDS

"I don't care what you say," my friend Steve Mayer said. "I think it stinks."

"Steve's right," Billy Alston said. "Your grandfather is a room robber and it isn't fair."

"By the way," Steve said, "I'm invading Quebec."

We were playing Risk, which is what we always played at Steve's house. Outside the living room window it was raining like crazy. Steve is a Risk fanatic, or expert, or both. Billy and I can never beat him. But today I was doing especially bad, maybe because I wasn't paying close attention.

Steve and Billy have been my friends ever since we met in kindergarten. Steve is taller than me and thinner and he wears these horn-rimmed eyeglasses. Maybe because he reads so much. Billy is a little shorter than both of us and he has crinkly red hair and thousands of freckles on his face. When Billy was six years old his dad hung a chinning bar in the doorway of his room. Whenever Billy goes in or out, he always chins himself a few times. Billy can do fifteen chin-ups. I know that because I once bet him he couldn't and lost a quarter. I can do three and a half chin-ups. Steve can hardly do one.

"Throw the dice," Steve said, and I did. I lost another army, of course, and Steve had one more territory of mine to control. Steve looked at me and shook his head. "You're such a dummy," he said.

"Look," I said, "he's my grandfather. What can I do?"

"Put up a fight," Steve said. "Stick up for your rights."

"I already have," I said.

"I won't let nobody take my room," Billy said. He made a fist and slammed it into his other palm. "Pow! Right in the nose!"

"Right, Billy," Steve said, winking at me. We both knew that Billy always talked tough like that, but the one time he had to face up to a kid in school called Phil Steinkraus he was as chicken as the rest of us.

"I'm trapped, don't you see?" I said. "I can't let my grandpa know how mad I am at losing my room. And if I can't even *talk* about it, what can I do?"

"Wishy-washy," Steve said. "What are you, a doormat?"

"You can't let a room robber walk all over you," Billy said.

Steve put down his fourth set of matched Risk cards and collected ten more armies. On the board he already controlled half the world, which meant the game wasn't going to last too much longer. He looked at me funny and then a slow grin started to spread all over his face. "Just got an idea," Steve said. "Yes, sir-ree, it just might work."

I waited while the wheels turned around in Steve's head.

"Seventeen seventy-six," Steve said.

Billy said, "Huh?"

"The Yankees against the power of the British army," Steve went on. "Here come the Red-coats, marching across a field in close formation. That's the way the British always fought. And what do the Minutemen do? They hide behind trees and rocks, they shoot from behind cover, and keep moving."

"What does this have to do with his grandpa?" Billy asked.

Steve sailed on. "Do you know that the British complained that the Minutemen didn't fight fair? *Fair?*"

"Steve—" I began.

"The legend of Zorro," Steve went on, "a rich and powerful man who fought the power of the king. He had to conceal his identity, because to fight against the king meant certain death. So what did he do to help the peasants against tyranny? He hid his face behind a mask."

"Like Batman and Robin," Billy said.

"Close," Steve said.

"What am I supposed to do?" I asked. "Get a sword and fight a duel? With Grandpa?"

"Gorilla warfare," Steve said, almost to himself. "When you're trapped and there's no other way. You fight from behind rocks. You conceal your identity."

"You're crazy," I said.

"It's the only way," Steve said. "Think about it."

13

A LIGHT
IN THE ATTIC

Gorilla warfare.

Hiding behind rocks and trees. Wearing a mask.

I was lying up in my bed and thinking about what Steve had said. It seemed crazy to me, and yet it made sense too. I was certainly trapped. My family had taken my room away and hadn't given me a chance to fight back.

Then I began to think about the people who fought in the Revolutionary days. Who were they fighting? The king. And the king was kind of a father to them, or maybe even a grandfather. He was certainly the biggest bigshot of 1776, that's for sure. And yet they fought for their rights. They took a chance and stood their ground at Lexington and Concord and fired the shot heard round the world.

But you don't shoot at your grandfather. Not in my family anyway.

It was hopeless.

But then I got a funny thought, and still another one. And the whole idea of what I could do became clear to me.

14

WAR IS DECLARED!!!

I scouted around and when nobody was looking sneaked down to my dad's office in the basement. It was a mess. There were three lights in the ceiling, but only one of them worked. Dad had put down the floor himself and some of the tiles were loose. There was a sink in the corner near the bathroom, but it didn't work and nobody knew how to fix it. Lucky for me, all I wanted was to use Dad's typewriter, and that was working.

When you start a war you have to send the enemy a note, or something like that, telling them what you want and why you want it. I had to let Grandpa know why I was about to go to war with him. And I really didn't want to sign my name to the note or even have it in my handwriting. Because if my parents got ahold of it, that would be the end of the war. And the end of me, probably.

I stuck a piece of my dad's scrap paper in his typewriter and began. Here's what I typed:

DECLARATION OF WAR!!!

YOU HAVE STOLEN SOMETHING THAT BE-LONGS TO ME. YOU HAVE TAKEN MY ROOM AND I WANT IT BACK. THIS IS A WARNING. YOU HAVE 24 HOURS TO GIVE ME BACK WHAT IS MINE. OR ELSE WAR WILL BEGIN.

I signed it this way: THE SECRET WARRIOR
I thought that was pretty good. The note sounded hard and tough. Like I really meant business. To tell the truth, I was so nervous, my hands were shaking. And then I thought Grandpa would certainly show it to Mom and Dad. So I put in a P.S. at the bottom.

P.S. THIS WAR IS BETWEEN YOU AND ME. DON'T TELL MY PARENTS OR I'LL NEVER TALK TO YOU AGAIN.

Well, I thought, if you are going to start a war, this note was a good way to begin. Now the question was, what should I do with it?
I thought about that for a long time. About

ten minutes anyway. I wanted to put it someplace where Grandpa could find it when he was
alone. I sure didn't want anyone else in the family to see it. That meant I had to put it in
Grandpa's room—*my* room, really, until he stole
it. And I had to sneak it in there sometime when
my mom wasn't coming up there to clean.

I waited until after dinner. All the time I
had that note folded up and tucked into my pants
pocket, which was practically the whole day, I
was like a shivery rabbit. Just feeling that piece
of paper crinkling in my pocket made me nervous.

I sneaked upstairs when Grandpa sat down
in front of the TV in the living room, which was
where he was almost every night now. I went
into Grandpa's room and closed the door quietly
behind me. Then I looked around. On top of the
dresser Grandpa had a photograph of Grandma
in an old silver frame. Next to it was his hair-
brush and comb. Then the door opened suddenly and I almost jumped out of my skin.

"Hi, Pete," Jenny said. "What are you
doing?"

"Nothing," I said real fast. My voice was so
high and squeaky, it sounded funny in my ears.

Jenny gave me a strange look. "Did I
frighten you?" she asked.

"No, you didn't frighten me," I lied.

"You look funny," she said, then shrugged. "You want to play casino? Mom and Dad are busy and Grandpa is too tired."

That was just like Jenny. Here I was about to start a war, and she wanted to play games.

"No, I don't want to play casino," I said, "or any other stupid game. Why don't you go downstairs and watch TV with Grandpa? Or read a book? Or go practice ballet? Or do anything instead of coming up here and bothering me?"

She looked at me for a long minute. "Weird," she said, "totally weird." Then she walked out of the room.

If this was how a war is, I thought, I wouldn't make a very good soldier. I took the folded note from my pocket, unfolded it, and stuck it under Grandpa's bedspread and on top of his pillow. He'd have to be blind not to see it. So he would surely read it tonight and then the war between us would start. I felt nervous about it, but not too much. Whatever was going to happen I was ready for.

Then I went upstairs to my stinky room and threw a tennis ball against the wall about forty million times.

15

IT TAKES TWO SIDES
TO FIGHT A WAR

Well, it was a lot of fear and worry over nothing. Because Grandpa didn't say anything or do anything about my note. Not the next day, anyway, or the day after that.

I didn't know what to do. Here I had declared war and written a note and my enemy totally ignored the whole thing. It looked like it was going to be the shortest war in history.

That day and the one after I followed Grandpa around and gave him plenty of chances to talk to me when nobody else was around. I even sat through a whole afternoon with him while he watched those stupid soap operas on TV. Later I went to the candy store with him when he wanted to buy some cigars. It took forever to walk two blocks, because Grandpa just limped along so slowly. "Is there anything you want to say to me?" I asked him on the way back.

He grinned at me. "Only that I like your company, Petey. You are very easy to be with."

"Isn't there something you read lately you want to talk about?" I asked. Like a note, I almost said.

"Just the newspaper," he said. "And there's so much bad news in it, I try not to pay too much attention."

I was learning something about Grandpa. He was one of the world's best ignorers. And my fight to get my room back looked like it would never even get started.

16

THE FIRST STRATEGY CONFERENCE

"You are so stupid, it's amazing you can live," Billy was saying. We were at his house, playing his game: Stratomatic Baseball. Steve and I had one team, Billy had the other. Naturally, Billy always fixed it so that he had Babe Ruth and Ty Cobb on his team. Naturally, Billy always seemed to win.

"You don't start a war with a note," Billy said. "You think the Japanese sent a note before they attacked Pearl Harbor? 'Dear United States, pardon us but we are going to sink all your ships. Sorry.'"

"Are you sure your grandfather got the note?" Steve asked.

"Yes. He couldn't miss it. It was right on his pillow."

"Maybe it fell out when he took the bedspread off," Steve said.

"Then where would it go?" I said. "On the

floor, out the window? It was a big piece of paper. It didn't just fly away."

"You have to attack," Billy said, "not just
write a polite note. Blam! Drop a bomb. Wham!
Hit him with a rocket."

"I am not going to bomb my grandpa," I
said.

"Then what are you going to do?" Steve said
in his slow and careful way. His eyes seemed to
be laughing at me as he waited for me to answer.

"I'll do something," I said.

"Some war," Billy said. Meanwhile, he
threw the dice and his All-Time All-Star team
scored two more runs on a double by Honus
Wagner. "It's time you got started fighting."

All of a sudden something clicked in my
head. Before I knew it, I began to laugh. Billy
and Steve looked at me as if I'd gone nuts.
"Thanks, Billy," I said, "thanks a lot. Time I got
started, all right. Time, sure enough."

And then I told them what I was going to
do.

17

NIGHT ATTACK

I really figured that I wouldn't be able to sleep at all that night, but I was wrong. I set my AM-FM digital clock-radio for two o'clock in the morning before I clicked off my reading lamp. I guess I must have tossed and turned for a while, thinking of what I was going to do and being nervous about it. But when the radio came on, playing a Beatles song, I was fast asleep.

I put the light on, shut off the radio, and looked at the note I had prepared one more time. This is what it said:

PEOPLE WHO STEAL OTHER PEOPLE'S ROOMS SHOULD NOT SLEEP WELL AT NIGHT. SURRENDER MY ROOM AND THE WAR WILL BE OVER.

THE SECRET WARRIOR

I took my pocket flashlight, put on my slippers, and went out into the hallway. Down the stairs to the second floor I sneaked, slow and careful, trying not to make any noise. The house was so quiet, it was weird. At the bottom of the stairs I paused for a moment; my heart was beating *thump-a-thump* very loud in my chest.

To tell you the truth, I felt uncertain about what I was about to do to Grandpa. But to get back what was mine, I had to fight. All's fair in love and war, somebody said. I hoped he wasn't the same guy who said Respect your elders.

I sneaked down the hallway like a thief in the night, tiptoeing past my parents' closed bedroom door and then Jennifer's. Outside of my old room I stepped around the floorboard that always creaked so loud. Then I turned the doorknob as slowly as I could, opened the door, and went into the room.

Even in the dark I could see that Grandpa was lying on his back under the covers, fast asleep. He was breathing slow and easy, making a little whistling noise that ended in a snore. One of his feet poked out of the covers at the bottom of the bed.

I walked very carefully around the floorboards I knew creaked and went to the dresser. Here was where I needed my pocket flash. I covered it with one hand and made sure the light went only on the little electric clock on top of the dresser.

This was the nasty part. I took the little clock and turned the alarm arrow so it pointed to three o'clock. I have to tell you that when the arrow went past two o'clock it made such a loud click I almost jumped a foot in the air. Be brave, Secret Warrior, I told myself. Then I pulled out the alarm button on the back of the clock, set down my note smack on top of the dresser where even a blind man could see it, and got myself out of the room in a hurry.

Upstairs I jumped into bed, turned out the light, and settled under the covers to see what was going to happen. In less than an hour, that alarm clock was going to go off, and Grandpa would be awakened in the middle of the night.

Be still my heart.

18

THE FIRST PEACE CONFERENCE

You know I couldn't fall asleep. It was kind of like waiting for a bomb to go off.

I watched the seconds and minutes flip down on my digital clock-radio. At 2:58 on my clock I heard the alarm clock go off in Grandpa's room downstairs. It sounded like an angry bee buzzing. And it kept buzzing for about a minute. Then I heard Grandpa get out of bed, and the alarm stopped.

Almost holding my breath, I waited. Now Grandpa would find the note. Then what would he do? Ignore me again?

I heard the sound of Grandpa's door opening. Was he coming up here? *Yes!* Now I could hear the creaking of the wooden stairs as his slippered feet came slow and limping upstairs. I got down under the covers and pretended to be asleep.

My door opened. I heard Grandpa come

across and stand next to my bed. "Pete?" he whispered. I kind of groaned a little, like I was asleep and having a dream. Grandpa sat down on the edge of the bed. I felt his hand on my shoulder, shaking me gently. "Pete? Come on, boy, I know you're not sleeping."

"Wha—what?" I said, like I was just coming awake. "Grandpa? Is that you?"

Grandpa reached over and snapped on my reading lamp. I shielded my eyes against the sudden glare. Grandpa's white hair was all mussed and he looked very angry. "Do you know what time it is?" he asked.

"Nighttime?"

"The middle of the night," he said, "*Mr. Secret Warrior*. It's not funny, Pete. I don't like someone playing tricks on me this way. Especially not my own grandson."

"It's not a trick," I said. "It's a war."

Grandpa shook his head. "Stuff and nonsense is what it is. You don't go to war against kin. You have to have an enemy to have a war, and I'm certainly not your enemy."

"You got my declaration of war," I said. "Why didn't you say anything about it?"

"I was kind of thinking it was a joke," Grandpa said.

"It's no joke," I said. "You took something of mine and I want it back."

"I didn't *take* anything," Grandpa said. "Your parents *gave* me your room, Pete."

"You've still got it, haven't you?" I said.

A funny look crossed Grandpa's face. "By God," he said, "you got a look on your face just like your mother when she was a kid. I hope you're not as stubborn as she was. She was a holy terror when she didn't get her way."

"I'm more stubborn," I said, "especially when I'm right."

Grandpa sighed, and stared at me for a minute. Then he slowly got to his feet. "Go back to sleep," he said. "We'll talk about this tomorrow. Which is almost here." He walked to the door.

"Grandpa," I called after him and he stopped in the doorway. "I love you," I said, which made him smile. *"But the war is still on!"*

19

A FLAG OF TRUCE

The next morning Grandpa didn't come down to breakfast until almost eleven o'clock. And he wasn't dressed, either, like he usually was. Mom gave him his breakfast of toast and coffee and he sat at the table eating it and reading the newspaper. He didn't even so much as say good morning to me, or anything, even though I was sitting right at the table with him.

On the other hand, he didn't tell Mom anything about what had happened during the night. I was glad about that.

In the afternoon Mom took Jennifer off to buy her some new shoes. I was outside the house, throwing a tennis ball against the front steps, when Grandpa came limping out to the porch. He watched me throw for a while, watched me fumble the ball a few times. "Soft hands," he said. "You've got to make your hands real soft when you catch a ball, Pete. Yours are too stiff and hard. Are you nervous about catching it?"

"Sure I am," I said, "seeing as how I drop it so much."

Grandpa grinned at that. "Soft hands are the secret, Pete," he said, then sat down in one of the porch chairs.

I threw some more as Grandpa watched, trying to do what he said. Maybe I caught the ball a little better, I'm not sure.

"Flag of truce?" Grandpa asked.

"What's that?"

"When two warring parties want to meet and talk things out, they put up a white flag of truce and then meet under it and have a powwow. How about it?"

"Okay," I said, and sat down on a chair next to him. "Does the white flag mean you're surrendering?"

"Certainly not. I just want to tell you a few things, okay?"

"Shoot," I said. "I mean, let's talk."

"Look, Peter, this situation is kind of out of my control, if you see what I mean." Grandpa looked down at his hands, which were big and knobby and had these little brown spots all over. "I didn't want to come up here from Florida and take your room. No way I wanted to do that. It's just the way things worked out, you understand?"

I nodded.

"I didn't want to retire from my business, for that matter," Grandpa said. "But when Grandma got sick, that's what I had to do. Didn't want to move to Florida, either, away from all the people I love. And I didn't want Grandma to die. It was lonely, rattling around in that house we had down there. Very lonely. So here I am and I guess you're stuck with me."

"I understand all that, Grandpa," I said.

"Good." He nodded.

"But I still want my room back."

"Oh, Petey," he said, kind of shaking his head. "I think maybe you are a little spoiled. Maybe because you've always had everything you want."

"I want only what's mine," I said.

"Single-minded," he said, "just like your mother. Your own room and everything. Let me tell you, when I was a boy I had to sleep in the same *bed* with your uncle Dave. Bad times, Petey, very hard times. We ate spaghetti a lot, and beans, and I never had two nickels to rub together. If I got a penny, it was a big thing. A penny meant I could go to the store and buy candy. And I sure took a lot of time deciding which candy. Now, look at you and Jenny. Great big house, lots of toys, good clothes, plenty to eat. You don't know about really wanting something, and doing without, do you?"

"I know I want my room. And you've got it."

"Stub-bor-in," Grandpa said, stretching the word out. "I think maybe it'll be good for you to do without, Petey. Really, I do."

"So you're not changing rooms with me?" I asked.

"Nope."

"Then the flag of truce is over," I said, getting up.

"Come on," Grandpa said, "don't be that way. Sit down."

"I've only got one thing to say," I told him as I walked off the porch. "Watch out for my second attack."

20

A SLIPPERY
CUSTOMER

What I did was steal Grandpa's slippers.

After dinner, on my way upstairs, I just stopped by my old room and took Grandpa's slippers from the bottom of the closet. I left a little note too. This one was written in Magic Marker on a sheet of notepaper. It said:

I WILL NOT
BE DEFEETED.
But you will.
The Secret Warrior

I had thought of doing some other tricky things to Grandpa. Like putting a frog in his bed. Or a gerbil. But then I thought maybe the surprise would really get him scared and maybe even give him a heart attack. That can happen to people, you know. Especially old people. They get a nasty shock and bingo—heart-attack city. I was at war with Grandpa, but I didn't want to kill him.

I went to bed thinking about all that, but before I fell asleep I heard footsteps coming up the stairs. Real slow and limpy footsteps.

Grandpa came in and snapped the overhead light on. "Okay," he said gruffly, "where are my slippers?"

"What slippers?" I said.

"The ones you stole, Petey-boy." Before I could answer he went over to my closet and opened it. There were his slippers in plain sight, right where yours truly was dumb enough to leave them. "My, my, what have we here?" Grandpa said. "Looks like somebody's slippers."

He picked them up and looked at me, shaking his head a little like he was disappointed. "Are we all finished with the sneaky tricks now?" he asked.

I didn't answer.

"You think you're one slippery customer, don't you?" he said. "Lots of tricks."

"Not tricks," I said.

"Oh, no? What would you call stealing my slippers then?"

"Gorilla warfare."

Grandpa looked at me, then began to laugh.

That really annoyed me. Here I was in the middle of a war and my enemy was laughing at me. "I don't think it's so funny," I said.

"Funnier than you think," Grandpa said. "Gorilla warfare, hah! *Monkeyshines* would be more like it."

"You've got your slippers," I said. "You can go now."

"Petey, we've got to get this settled between us. Tomorrow, maybe. You go to sleep now, okay, but tomorrow we talk." He leaned down over my bed and gave me a dry kiss on my forehead. "Good night," he said.

"Good night," I said back to him. I wanted to say more, like I was sorry, but I didn't. A war is a war, I thought, and it does not end until one party surrenders.

"Gorilla warfare," he said on the way out of my room. When he closed the door he was chuckling to himself.

It was then I began to think that I would probably lose the war. Grandpa was so nice, he would just ignore everything I did. And in the end he would stay in my room and I'd be stuck up here forever.

Some war this is, I thought. My enemy just kissed me good night.

21

STRATEGY
AND SUPPLIES

"That's very revealing, you know," Steve was saying as we walked to the store. "He actually kissed you."

"Yes," I said.

"It's psychological warfare," Steve said, "and very clever of him."

"He's messing with your mind," Billy said.

We were on our way to Dealtown, the store where we always bought school supplies. Steve needed more pens, index cards, and a notebook. I never knew a kid who used up so many school supplies as Steve did, or who loved school as much as he did. It was a little unnatural, if you ask me. I mean, school is okay. And besides, you have to go. But I always think that a few more holidays during the year wouldn't hurt anything. Steve thinks that a day without school is a rotten day. He's always reading books and taking notes on index cards. Whenever he sees a new word he looks it up in the dictionary, writes it on an index card, and memorizes it.

"Grandpa is trying to out-nice you," Steve said.

"But he is nice," I said.

"There you are," Steve said. "He's got you believing it already."

"Wait a minute," I said, "something's wrong here."

"Yeah, *you* are," Billy said.

"It's very simple," said Steve as we entered the store. "You start a war, Grandpa doesn't want to fight. So he just tries to be so darn nice to you that you'll forget the whole thing and call off the war. Isn't that it?"

"No," I said. "He's just a good sweet man who loves me a lot. So he forgave my stealing his slippers and let me know by kissing me."

"That wasn't too bright, leaving his slippers in your closet," Billy said. "You should have thrown them in the trash."

"I'd never do that," I said.

"Or burned them," Billy added.

"You can't burn slippers," I said.

"Positively Machiavellian," Steve said. He picked up a shopping basket.

"What's Machia—what you said?" Billy asked.

"Machiavelli. He was this old Italian prince," Steve said. "He figured out all the moves you can make on an enemy a long time ago. I'll bet your grandpa knows all about him." Steve put a spiral-bound notepad and a pack of index cards into the basket.

"He's not that way," I protested. "Grandpa is just a great guy, that's all."

Steve gave me one of those all-knowing looks of his, as if he were talking to a birdbrain. "Never underestimate your enemy," he said.

I have to say this about my friend Steve. Sometimes for a guy who is a great brain and all, he can be very dumb.

"So what are you going to do next?" Billy asked.

"Probably nothing," Steve said.

"You're both wrong," I said. "I'll do something. I still want my room back."

"Can you put a lock on the door so he can't get in?" Billy wanted to know.

"No," I said.

Steve took a ten-pack of ball-point pens and put it into his basket. "I'll tell you what I think," he said. "I think the war is over . . . and you've lost."

22

SLAPSHOT

When I came out on the porch after lunch, Grandpa was waiting. "Let's meander," he said to me. "I figure we have some talking to do."

"What about your leg?"

"Well," Grandpa said, "it's still attached to my body."

"I mean, doesn't it hurt when you walk a lot?"

"Petey," he said, "it hurts when I walk and also when I don't walk. So maybe I ought to get some exercise and the heck with my leg."

We began to walk toward Beverly Road, the shopping street a few blocks away. "Is this a flag of truce?" I asked.

"There you go with that war business again," Grandpa said. "Forget that."

"I'm not forgetting," I said. "I declared war on you and I mean it."

"Pish-tosh," Grandpa said. I didn't know

what that meant, exactly, but I kind of got the idea. "This isn't a war," he said. "It's a disagreement. Maybe even a dispute. And what you're doing is starting a family feud."

"It is too a war," I insisted. "You moved in and took over my territory, didn't you? Isn't that what wars are about?"

"No," said Grandpa. "Wars are about power and greed."

"And getting back what's yours," I said.

Grandpa stopped walking and I stopped too. His eyes seemed hard and cold when they looked at me. "So you think war is perfectly okay," he said. "Is that about it?"

"Sometimes," I said.

"Like when?"

"When you have to stick up for your rights," I said.

Grandpa's mouth made a thin line as he shook his head. "That's wrong, Petey. There are lots of ways of settling arguments without going to war. Peaceful ways."

"I tried that with my parents. It didn't work. That's why I had to go to war with you."

"Wrong," Grandpa said.

"Not wrong," I said back to him. "You took my room."

"Listen, Pete," Grandpa said slowly. "The only time you have to fight a war is when someone attacks you. Then, and only then, you have a right to defend yourself. You got that?"

I thought about that for no more than a second. "Wasn't I attacked?" I said. "Didn't they yank me out of my room and shove me away upstairs like I was some old chair or something?"

Grandpa sighed and looked away for a minute. I could see he was upset.

"It's just like Risk," I said. "Someone invades your territory, you zap them."

I felt Grandpa's bony hand on my arm. "War is no game, Petey," he said. "Only kids and fools and generals think that."

"You're my enemy," I said in a loud voice, "and I want what's mine."

I shook his hand off my arm. "You marched in here like an army and kicked me out of—"

WHACK!

Grandpa's right hand came whipping out of nowhere and slapped me hard across my cheek. I was so shocked and surprised, I couldn't say anything. My cheek felt hot and burning. It hurt.

"Why'd you hit me?" I said. I had tears in my eyes, but I didn't cry.

"War hurts," Grandpa said. "War wounds

and kills and causes misery. Only a fool wants war."

I stared into Grandpa's brown eyes that looked so mean to me now. "I won't forget this," I said.

"That's the idea."

"And I won't forgive it either. From now on we're *really* at war." I turned away and started back to the house, walking as fast as I could. I left Grandpa on the street, calling my name.

23

TIME OUT
FOR JENNY

Well, now we had a real war going and I didn't like it one little bit. I'm really not too good at being mad at someone. My mom says I have a good heart and never hold a grudge. This is true. Even in the past, when my parents or Jenny did something that ticked me off, I always forgot about it by the next day.

So there I was at dinner that night, sitting across from Grandpa, and I really wanted to hate him for slapping me but I couldn't. I mean, he was my *grandfather*, for heaven's sake. He was old and alone and his leg hurt him. I would have to be as mean as Darth Vader to hate him.

Grandpa was really lively at dinner. He even told a couple of jokes nobody had heard before. He smiled and talked to me, too, but I couldn't tell if he really meant it or not. Was this the same man who had slapped me across the face only a few hours ago? I was confused.

So we had a regular evening that night, in spite of the mixed-up feelings I had. After dinner we settled down in the living room. Grandpa got out his box of dominoes and began to set them up for a game with Dad. Jenny disappeared for a few minutes, then came marching down the steps from her room wearing her tutu. In case you have never heard that word before, which I never did until Mom bought her one, let me tell you about a tutu. It's this little skirt that must have wires or something in it because it sticks out in a circle when a girl wears it. Jenny's was pink. How she got it was by being obnoxious. Because Mom didn't want to buy it for her, not until she had more than one year of ballet lessons. But Jenny is very different from me. I'm the kind of person who would have waited for a year, just like Mom said.

Not Jenny.

She went on a campaign for a tutu that was disgusting. She talked about it morning, noon, and night. She cried when she had to go for her ballet lessons. She told Mom that all the girls had a tutu, which was a lie, of course.

She even threw herself down on the floor and had a tantrum. I mean she kicked her heels on the floor and yelled her head off until Mom finally made her quit. When that didn't succeed, Jenny went to work on Dad. She got him alone at all different times, climbed up on his lap, and smothered him with kisses like a puppy licking your face. She just kept sweet-talking Dad and being so lovey-dovey to him, it could make you sick. So what happened was Dad spoke to Mom, and Jenny got her tutu. And it wasn't even Christmas or her birthday.

Jenny went to the stereo and put on her record of The Dance of the Hours.

"Ladies and gentlemen," she announced like she was on a stage, "presenting the world's most beautiful ballerina—Miss Jennifer Stokes!" Then she let the record begin, which we had heard maybe fourteen zillion times already. But Mom, Dad, and Grandpa—especially Grandpa— sat back and applauded like they had never seen Jenny dance before.

What she did was jump around on her toes a lot. Every once in a while she stretched her arms way up over her head like she was trying to reach a shelf in her closet. Sometimes she kind of stood around on one foot with the other leg trailing off behind her. Posing that way, she looked like a small stork or a large chicken. Also she hopped. She was supposed to leap, I think, but Jenny could manage to get only a few inches off the floor. At the end she scrunched herself into a bundle on her knees, then lifted her arms and smiled as the music ended.

Well, of course, the grown-ups went bananas when she finished. "Bravo!" Dad shouted as they all applauded. I noticed he didn't shout "Encore!" I applauded, too, mostly to be polite.

Sometimes it's very hard to be an older brother.

24

A DIRTY TRICK

I think I was finally getting a little smarter about my war with Grandpa. Perhaps I had been following the advice of friends too much. And maybe I had been telling them too much about what was going on. Blabbing my head off would be more like it. So when Steve and Billy came by to play Monopoly at my house, I didn't tell them anything about the slap in the face from Grandpa.

Let me tell the truth about it. I was also a little ashamed.

We were all upstairs in my room. My new horrible and totally gross room, not my old wonderful and beautiful room.

"So this is where they put you," Steve said, looking around. "It's not an improvement."

"It stinks," Billy said.

"I'm getting used to it," I said.

"Any action?" Billy asked.

I shook my head.

"The war is over," Steve said, "just as I predicted."

"You're a loser," Billy said. He was sitting on the floor on the little braided rug in front of my bed. "I liked your old room better. It was roomier. And it had more light. And it didn't have a smell."

"Smell?" I said. "What smell?"

"Don't you smell it?" Billy asked. He wrinkled his nose like a rabbit and sniffed.

"It smells okay," I said. "Steve, you don't smell anything, do you?"

Steve took a breath through his nose. "Yes," he said.

We waited for a moment, looking at Steve, but he didn't say anything more. "Yes, you do, or yes, you don't?" Billy asked.

"I smell something, of course," Steve said. "My olfactory sense is working."

"Your old factory *what*?" Billy asked. "I don't smell an old factory. More like some kind of cheese."

"Olfactory," Steve said. "O-l-f-a-c-t-o-r-y. Your nose and smelling glands, your sense of smell."

"Oh," Billy said. "You mean you're showing off your vocabulary again."

"Precisely," Steve said, grinning. "Or indubitably . . . or . . ."

"Let's play Monopoly," I said before it went any further. Sometimes Steve could be a pain in the neck. And sometimes he really teased Billy too much.

I went to my toy cabinet and took out the Monopoly game. Steve sat down on the floor next to Billy. "I'll be banker," I said.

"Of course," Billy said.

"Pete is always banker," Steve said, "and he always wins."

"What does that mean?" I said.

Steve shrugged. "Nothing," he said in a way that sounded like it meant a lot more than nothing.

"Can we just play, for Pete's sake!" Billy said.

I sat down on the floor with the guys and set the game down in front of me. Then I took off the cover. Then I saw something so unbelievable, I couldn't believe it.

The Monopoly board was in the box, all right, but nothing else was.

There was no money, no playing pieces, no properties, no rules. All there was was a folded piece of paper. I unfolded it. It was a note, printed with a ball-point pen. This is what it said:

TWO CAN PLAY AT THIS GAME.
BUT YOU CAN'T PLAY THIS GAME NOW.

Down below it was signed: THE OLD MAN.

25

AND DIRTY WORDS

I will not put down here the actual words that Billy and Steve said. I know I set out to tell this story like it happened, but I don't want to put those words down on paper. Especially in a story for my teacher to read.

So I will make up some words to use instead of the real ones.

"I can't believe this," Billy said. "What a *gribetz mcplank* think to do!"

"Exactly," Steve said, "it's *rorvish!*"

"Only a *macnishtop* would pull a *furrzy* trick like this!" Billy said.

"Wait a minute," I said. "And don't say that about my grandpa."

"I'll say what I like," Billy said. He was really mad. "He's a *macnishtop*. How can you deny it?"

"He is not a *macnishtop!*" I said in a loud voice. "My grandpa is a great guy."

"And he pulls *furrzy* tricks," Steve said.

Steve had me there. It was pretty *furrzy* all right. "Maybe," I said. "But I sure have given him a couple of reasons for it. I started this war, don't forget."

Well, the guys went on and on for a while, saying some more *rorvish* things about Grandpa. And I defended him. It took some time for all of us to simmer down. Then Steve got that funny look on his face and shut up while Billy ran down at the mouth.

"It may be terrific," Steve said then.

"What's so terrific about it?" Billy asked.

"He has risen to the bait, don't you see?" said Steve. "I mean, he's in the game now, he wants to play. And that's good."

"We can't play Monopoly now and you say it's good," said Billy.

"You've got your grandpa involved now," Steve said, ignoring Billy. "He's feeling the pressure. Now you've got to keep it up."

"How?" I said.

"Attack, attack, attack," Steve said.

"Yeah," Billy said, "hit him again."

"I'm not so sure," I said. I really wasn't sure either.

"Burn his underwear!" Billy said.

"What?" I didn't think I heard Billy right.

"Sneak in, grab all his underwear, and burn it. A man can't go anywhere without his underwear."

"And how do you burn underwear?" I asked sarcastically.

"Throw it in the furnace," Billy said.

"Don't be stupid," I said. I wouldn't go anywhere near our furnace for anything, much less throw underwear into it.

"Rip it up then," Billy said. "Just throw it in the trash. But do it."

"Not on your life," I said.

"You're not a Secret Warrior," Billy said. "You're a chicken."

"I'm a grandson," I said. "There are some things I'm not going to do, no matter how much my friends egg me on."

"Chicken!" Billy said.

"It's not your war," I said.

"*Gribetz Mcplank!*" Billy called me, which he knows I don't like. I didn't say anything back.

"You've got to do something," Steve said.

"I will," I said.

"What?" Steve asked.

"I don't know."

"When?"

"Sometime, someplace," I said.

Steve and Billy both laughed at me then. And in a little bit they left, both of them mad at me and me annoyed with them.

So Grandpa's first attack really worked after all. It took three good friends and made them *rorvish* with each other.

26

ROCKER AND ROLL

You can bet your life I went looking for Grandpa right after the boys left. But he was too clever for me. He hung around in the kitchen where Mom was preparing dinner. Then he played a few hands of casino with Jenny. By that time Dad was home from the office.

I didn't get to speak to him alone and in private until after school the next day. And he was up in my room when I got home. He had his big toolbox up there and he was sitting on my bed, carving a little piece of wood with his knife. "Hello, Pete," he said in a friendly way, "how was school today?"

I put my knapsack down. "A lot you care," I said.

"I care, I care," Grandpa said.

"How did you know we were going to play Monopoly?" I asked him.

"Ah-ah." He grinned. "A military secret."

"I suppose you think it was funny."

Grandpa chuckled. "Wasn't it? Here you guys get together to play a game and *surprise*!" Grandpa took the little piece of wood and knelt down next to my rocking chair. Then he tried to fit it into the hole in the back of the chair where the arm kept coming loose. "Just a touch too big," he said.

"You're fixing my rocker," I said.

"Trying to," Grandpa said. He had a piece of sandpaper and was rubbing that little piece of wood like crazy.

"Are you going to glue it again?" I asked.

"Nope," said Grandpa. "Glue won't do it. I'm repegging it, Pete. You see this hole in the back of the arm? I took the old peg out. It used to fit in this other hole here in the back of the rocker." Grandpa tried to put the little piece of wood into place, but it wouldn't fit. "Just a little more sanding now," he said.

"What about all the stuff from my Monopoly game? Can I have it back now?"

"Not until," he said.

"Until what?"

"Until our little disagreement, or whatever you want to call it, is over."

I looked at Grandpa, but he was busy sanding. "I don't think that's fair," I said.

"It's not," he said. "Let's just say your Monopoly pieces are prisoners of war. As soon as we make peace, back they come."

"I'll never do that. Not until you give up my room."

"Then they'll stay prisoners a long time," Grandpa said.

He took a pair of pliers and gripped them around the middle of the wooden peg. Then he stuck it into the arm hole and kind of twisted it while pushing all the time. It took a lot of effort, but Grandpa had big hands and big muscles and it finally went into the hole about halfway. "Got it," Grandpa said, "solid as the Rock of Gibraltar."

"I gave you back your slippers," I said.

"It seems to me that I had to come up here and find those slippers myself," he said. "I didn't see you hand them over, Pete."

I thought about that while Grandpa put the pliers away and got out a hammer from the toolbox. The hammer had a rubber tip on the hitting part.

"I'm going to have to get you back for this," I said. "The Secret Warrior will strike again."

"I know that," Grandpa said, grinning. "That's the fun of it."

I couldn't believe he'd said that. "You think it's fun?"

"Sure is," he answered. "Oh, it took me a-while to see it. And then I realized something. I had darn near lost my whole sense of humor. Hadn't had a good time for ages and ages. Not the last year anyway. Imagine me slapping you like that. What a fool thing to do." He lined up the hole in the back of the rocker with the peg that was stuck in the arm. "Now, watch this, Pete old boy."

Tap-tap-tap! That's all it took, three good taps with Grandpa's hammer and the arm of the rocker was attached to the back. I sat right down in the rocker and tried it out. It was solid, just like Grandpa said.

"You're a good fixer," I said. "Thanks." I kissed his forehead.

"I'm the best," Grandpa said. "You know, Pete, I used to build whole *houses* from the bottom up. Still would, if it wasn't for this bum leg. But I'm starting to feel good again. Got my old pizzazz back, I think. There's lots of things in this house that need fixing. And I'm the man for the job, kiddo."

He gave me a hug then, and it felt good. But when he let me go I looked at him and said,

"I'm going to get you for that Monopoly trick, you know."

"Sure you will," he said, then he laughed. "I can hardly wait."

27

GO FISH

I was thinking pretty hard about how I was going to get back at Grandpa. It wasn't easy. There were a lot of things I could do and a lot I'd never do. Like burning his underwear, for instance. I didn't want to do something I'd be sorry for later.

I thought about, and then actually tried to steal his toolbox and hide it. But I found the thing was so big and heavy that just thinking about carrying it up three flights of stairs from the basement to hide it in the attic was enough to make me tired.

Then I figured out what I'd do. But before I had a chance to do it, I spent a day with Grandpa I want to tell about.

On Friday night Grandpa asked me if I'd ever gone fishing. I told him no, I hadn't. Dad was not a fisherman. And the only time I ever saw a live fish was in the big tank at the fish store. Unless you count the lobster I saw once in a restaurant, but he was cooked. Or the gold-fish I had once for about a week until he died.

"Well," Grandpa said, "I'm thinking about going out tomorrow morning to catch us a mess of flounder. I'd sure appreciate the company, Petey. And I think you'd like it too."

I wasn't so sure I'd like it. "You won't go out in the ocean, will you?" I asked.

"Nope, just a couple of hundred yards from shore in Cold Spring Harbor."

"Where's that?"

"A short ride away. Maybe thirty miles or so."

"We wouldn't run into anything big and dangerous, would we?"

"Like what?" Grandpa asked.

"Like Jaws."

Grandpa laughed. "Well, now," he said, "I never thought of that. I don't think we'll meet up with Jaws, Petey. Leastways, I never have in all the times I fished out there."

"Okay, then," I said, feeling relieved.

Grandpa told me we'd be getting up very early the next day, but when he told me to set my alarm for four thirty A.M. I couldn't believe it. "That's the middle of the night," I said.

"You've got to get up pretty early to out-smart a flounder," he said.

Did you ever get up and out of bed at four thirty in the morning? It's pitch-black outside then. I washed and dressed and put on all the clothing Grandpa said I'd need. Old jeans, T-shirt, a flannel shirt, an old sweater over that, and my hooded sweat-shirt jacket to go on top. Grandpa was down in the kitchen working on a bunch of sandwiches to take along. "Ham and bologna," he said, "that okay with you?"

"Fine," I said, "no mustard on mine."

"Okay," he said. "You should never take tuna or any other fish sandwiches when you go out fishing. Scares away the fish."

"How could that be?" I asked.

"Don't know," said Grandpa, "but I believe it."

He put the bag of sandwiches into a vinyl zipper bag along with a thermos of cold milk for me. He had another big old thermos he said we'd fill with hot coffee on the way. If you're hungry, Grandpa told me, take some bread or crackers, because we weren't going to eat break-fast for an hour or so. I told him I wasn't hungry. What I was was sleepy.

We stepped out onto the front porch into

the black morning. I peeked into the milk box near the door. "The milkman wasn't even here yet and we're leaving," I said. "Why do we have to go fishing so early?" I asked. "Won't the fish be there in the afternoon too?"

"Tides," Grandpa said as we went to Mom's car. Before I got into the front seat I squinted up into the black sky. The stars looked like asterisks.

Grandpa drove slowly and carefully through city streets, then turned onto the Interstate highway. "High tides," Grandpa explained to me, "are when most of the fish like to feed. The water comes into the harbor and it brings a lot of things fish like to eat. So if you drop your hook on the incoming tide, see, Mr. Fish just thinks, 'Here's a tasty nibble,' and takes your bait. That's why we have to be out and on the water by seven o'clock today. Because the high tide comes at 9:07 exactly." He looked over at me in the dark. "You do know what a tide is, don't you?"

"It's when the water gets higher and lower," I said. "But what makes it do that?"

"The moon," Grandpa said.

I thought he was making a joke. "How about the stars?" I said. "Or mountains or trees, maybe?"

Grandpa chuckled. "Nope, just the moon. And on the full moon you get your highest tides of the month. It's called gravitational pull, Pete, and it's true. You could look it up sometime. People keep charts of tides and they can tell you when each tide will come for years and years ahead. The tide is very important."

"Must be," I said. "It pulled me right out of bed at four thirty in the morning, didn't it?"

We stopped at a diner a little while later and had breakfast. It was only about five o'clock in the morning, the earliest I ever had breakfast in my life. Grandpa had the waitress fill his thermos with coffee and we hit the road again.

Grandpa was humming along with a song on the radio. He seemed very happy. Ahead of us the sky was beginning to lighten as dawn came up. "Ain't it great?" Grandpa grinned at me. "Just us two gents out on the road, footloose and fancy-free. Don't you love it?"

It did feel good being out and alone with Grandpa.

We got to Cold Spring Harbor just as the sun was peeping all red and gold at the edge of the sky. Grandpa drove down to the water and parked near Bill's Boat and Bait Shop. I have to tell something true right here. Inside that place it smelled so awful, there ought to be a law against it. It smelled like rotten fish had been left there for about a year. That smell could gross out my whole class. Maybe the whole school.

We got two little pails of bait and walked down the dock on the other side to where the rowboats were tied up. Grandpa helped me into my life vest and put one on himself. Then we put all our stuff into the boat. It had a wide, flat bottom, and Grandpa tucked our fishing rods and tackle under the front seat, then helped me get in. "Safety first," he told me. "No standing up, sit in one place on the seat, and tell me beforehand if you want to move around."

"Aye, aye, sir," I said, and it made him grin.

Grandpa untied us from the dock, put the oars into place, and rowed us out into the harbor. It was neat, traveling across the smooth water in a small boat, the sunlight dancing on the water and a cool breeze in my face. "I love it," I said to Grandpa and he smiled.

There's a whole lot more to tell about that day, but this chapter is much too long already. I could tell about Grandpa teaching me to bait a hook with a worm or a piece of dead clam. About how you drop your hook until you feel the bottom and then take up just enough slack in your line. Or the fantastic feeling when a flounder takes the bait and starts to wiggle and jump around, and how you have to pull him in so careful and slow, and getting him up and into the boat.

Almost everything about that day was wonderful. We caught a whole lot of fish, more than twenty. I got so hungry, I ate my first sandwich before nine o'clock. I learned how to row a boat. It was hard to do, but I rowed us partway back to the dock. I learned how to clean a fish and get the scales off.

It was an adventure. Exciting, thrilling, and just a little bit of danger behind it. And I loved every minute of it.

"We're going to do this again," I told Grandpa on the way home.

"You bet we are," he said.

And we have gone fishing together a lot, many times since that first day. Once we even took Jenny along and she liked it too. But nothing will ever make me forget that first time alone with Grandpa.

So you can see why I felt a little sad later that night when I sneaked into my old room and stole Grandpa's wristwatch.

28

PLAYING HARDBALL

It did not take Grandpa too long to discover that his watch was missing. And I guess he didn't have to walk around trying to figure out where it had gone.

He came upstairs the next morning. It was a Sunday and I was waiting around for Mom and Dad to wake up so I could go downstairs for breakfast. I heard Grandpa coming and grabbed a book so I could be pretending to read.

Grandpa knocked on my door ever so lightly, then pushed it open a crack to look in. "Awake, I see," he said. He came in and sat down in my rocker. He was wearing his pajamas, robe, and slippers. "A funny thing happened this morning," he said. "I went to slip my watch on and guess what? It seemed to be missing from my dresser."

"Is that so?" I said in a casual way.

"That's a fact."

"Well," I said, "maybe there was a thief who came into the house last night and stole it."

"Don't think so," Grandpa said. "Seeing as how my wallet was on the dresser, too, right next to my watch, and it wasn't even touched. I had quite a few dollars in it too."

"Maybe it was a very dumb thief," I said. "Or a thief who needed only a watch."

Grandpa looked at me and grinned. I didn't blame him. What I'd said sounded stupid to me too. "How come you didn't leave a note?" Grandpa said.

"I think we're past all that," I said.

"Maybe so."

"I took your watch," I said. "We both know that."

Grandpa kind of shook his head a little. "I was kind of thinking maybe our little war was over," he said. "Especially after yesterday. I had a good time fishing with you, Pete. You're very good company."

"Well," I said, "it wasn't your average kind of day for me either. I had one of the best days of my life with you. But—" I said, and sort of shrugged. "It doesn't change things, Grandpa."

"So I see."

"There's something I want and you have

and I don't know what else to do except fight for what's mine," I said.

"Too bad," Grandpa said. "But look, Petey, I have a special reason for wanting my watch back. It was a gift from Grandma, you see, on our fortieth wedding anniversary. I treasure it, son."

Well, now I felt like the most miserable low-down person in the whole wide world. But I wasn't about to give up. "It's in a safe place, Grandpa," I said. "And I'll take good care of it."

I didn't have to take care of it at all. Because it was wrapped up nice and snug in a pair of my white socks and hidden away in a tennis ball can in the bottom of my camp trunk.

"I could probably find it if I looked," Grandpa said.

"I don't think so," I said.

"I'm pretty good at looking," Grandpa said. "When you're in school, Pete, I've got all day to turn this place over."

"You could look for a million years and never find it," I said.

Grandpa sighed and rocked a few times in the chair. "I'd rather you handed it back by yourself," he said.

"No way," I said. "Not until you give me my room back."

"I've heard that before," he said. "How about if I say please?"

"Look, Grandpa," I said, "all you have to do is tell Mom and Dad that you want to switch rooms with me. That's easy, isn't it?"

Grandpa took a long look in my eyes, rocking so gently in my chair. "You're really like a broken record, you know that?" he said.

"I only want what's rightly mine," I said.

"So," Grandpa said, "now we're playing hardball, eh?"

"I'm not playing," I said. "No room . . . no watch."

"Fair enough," Grandpa said. He got up and slowly walked to the door. "But from now on," he said, "you'd better watch out."

29

WAITING FOR THE OTHER SHOE TO DROP

Did you ever know something terrible was going to happen but you didn't know when?

That's the way I felt that whole time when Grandpa waited before striking back at me. It was real smart of him. Diabolical, if you want to know the truth. I walked around going crazy for about a week. I mean, it's hard to be calm when someone is going to do something to you and you don't know what it is or when it is going to happen.

I lay awake without sleeping a few nights, wondering when the blow was going to come down. It reminded me of this story about an old Greek guy named Damocles who went to a party where they hung a sword over his head by a hair. It had to be either a very skinny sword or a very fat hair. But either way it couldn't have been too comfortable to be waiting for that sword to come down and slice you into human chicken parts.

I felt like I was in the dentist's office, waiting my turn, wondering how much it was going to hurt. It's the same feeling I get in school just before a test when everything I studied just jumps out of my head. You could ask me my own name just before a test and I might not know it.

And Grandpa was teasing me, which didn't help a bit.

"You look nervous," he'd say.

"I am, for goodness' sakes," I'd say. "I wish you'd do something already."

"Patience," he'd say with a funny smile that gave me a chill.

Psychological warfare, right? I mean, he was messing with my mind. And the more he waited, the more messed up I got. I left one of my schoolbooks home one day. Just plain forgot it. I knew why. Because I was too busy worrying over what kind of trick he was going to pull on me.

Grandpa told me a joke one afternoon. It was about a guy who lived below a man who took off only one shoe when he got into bed at night. The man below couldn't hardly sleep, waiting for the other shoe to drop.

I didn't think it was very funny.

30

JENNY THE SPY

Right around then, while I was waiting for the other shoe to drop, a peculiar thing happened. It was a rainy Sunday. Mom was in the kitchen baking something with cinnamon in it that made the whole house smell terrific. Jenny was helping. After a while Jenny must have helped too much because Mom sent her out of the kitchen. Grandpa was sitting in the living room with me. Dad was upstairs taking a nap.

Next thing Grandpa and I knew, Jenny came walking into the room with my Monopoly game. My empty Monopoly game with all the pieces and cards hidden away by Grandpa. "Let's play," Jenny said. She set the game down on the coffee table.

"Ahem," Grandpa said, kind of coughing.

"Where'd you get that?" I said. I acted like I was mad.

"From your toy cabinet," Jenny said, "where

you always keep it." She began to open the box, but I stopped her by putting my hand on top of it.

"Don't you ask permission to go into my room and steal my game?" I said real loud.

Jenny looked at me in a funny way. "What do you mean, *steal* it?" she said. "Here it is. I think we should play Monopoly. You, me, and Grandpa."

"That's a stupid idea," I said.

Jenny blinked her eyes at me. "What's the matter with you, Peter?" she asked. "You're acting funny."

"I don't want to play Monopoly, okay?" I said. "I have my rights, you know, and if a person doesn't want to play Monopoly, a person can't be forced against his will. So I'll just put the game away."

I didn't expect Jenny to jerk the box away, but she did. And then she opened it. "I'll play with Grandpa then, if you're going to be so mean," she said.

I looked at Grandpa and he looked at me. We both knew what was coming next.

"Hey, where are all the pieces and cards and stuff?" Jenny asked. "There's just a Monopoly board and nothing else in the box."

There was a very long and very embarrassing silence. Jenny stared at me and at Grandpa. I couldn't think of what to say. Grandpa began to whistle.

And then Jenny found the note I'd stupidly left in the box.

" 'Two can play at this game,' " she read aloud, " 'but you can't play this game now.' Signed, 'The Old Man'?" She looked mystified. "Who is The Old Man?" she asked. "And why are the pieces missing?"

"Well," I said, "there's a perfectly simple explanation."

Jenny waited. I waited, too, because I couldn't think of a perfectly simple explanation.

"Something fishy is going on here," Jenny said.

Grandpa cleared his throat.

"You both know about this and I don't," Jenny said. "Are you The Old Man in the note, Grandpa? Are you playing a trick on Peter?"

"Me?" Grandpa said. "*Me?* Don't be silly. Why would I play a trick on Peter?"

Jenny thought about that for no more than a second. "It *is* you, Grandpa. That's why you look so guilty. I wish you'd tell me. You know I can keep a secret."

"Stuff and nonsense," Grandpa said in a huffy

way, like he was being insulted. "One of Pete's
friends did this, I'll bet. Isn't that right, Pete?"

"Huh?" I said. "Yeah . . . right."

"Who?" asked Jenny.

"The older one," Grandpa said.

"That's right," I said. "Steve did it. He's a
lot older than me. And sometimes he calls himself the old man."

"Steve isn't a lot older than you," Jenny
said. She would make a great detective, I was
thinking.

"Sure he is," I said. "Months and months."

"So where did Steve hide all the Monopoly
pieces?" Jenny asked. "Why don't you get them,
Peter, so we can play, okay?"

"Well . . ." I said.

"You go upstairs and get them, Pete," said
Grandpa, who stood up from the couch. "And
I'll just step up to my room and get me a sweater.
It's kinda chilly in here."

Now I understood what was happening. So
I ran up to my room like I was getting the Monopoly stuff while Grandpa retrieved it from
wherever he had hidden it. I met him outside
my old room. "A narrow escape there," he said.
He handed me a plastic bag with all the Monopoly stuff in it.

And I handed him back his watch.

"Thanks," he said, and slipped the watch onto his wrist.

"This doesn't mean I'm giving up," I told him.

"Course not," Grandpa said. "And I still owe you one, I believe. I'm going to drop the other shoe on you any day now."

Then we went back downstairs and played Monopoly with Jenny until dinnertime.

31

THE SHOE DROPS ...
KERPLUNK!

When it happened, I wasn't ready for it, of course. It was an ordinary Wednesday in the middle of the week. A school day. The first thing I noticed was that my clock-radio alarm hadn't gone off at the right time. I always get up at seven o'clock. But it was already seven fifteen!

I leaped out of bed, tangling my feet in the blanket and falling onto the floor. Next thing I noticed was that my slippers were gone. I always leave them right alongside my bed when I go to sleep. Why weren't they there?

I wasted a minute or two looking for them under the bed and in my closet. That's when it hit me. *This was Grandpa's revenge!* Now. This morning. That's why the clock was late and my slippers were gone.

I rushed off to the bathroom in my bare feet to wash my face and brush my teeth. No tooth-brush! It simply wasn't there. In the plastic water glass on the sink was a note. "Use your finger," it said.

What a *furrzy* trick!

I stood there like a dummy, half of me wanting to run downstairs to the hall closet where Mom kept a few new toothbrushes and half of me not wanting to waste the time because I was already behind schedule. I put toothpaste on my finger and brushed my teeth with it. It was disgusting.

I ran back to my room in a hurry. I hate being late for anything, but I hate being late for school most of all. When I opened my underwear drawer it was empty.

There was another note. This one said: "Underwear in hall closet." I ran outside into the hall. There was all my underwear, up on a shelf. I grabbed shorts and a T-shirt and ran back to my room and put them on. That's when I looked into my sock drawer. And that's when I saw it was empty too.

Now I was mad. In a panic, yes, but mad as well. The note in my sock drawer said: "Socks in cabinet under bathroom sink."

I groaned and said a couple of words I shouldn't use. Grandpa was turning my getting dressed into a treasure hunt. I ran to the bath-

room again and looked under the sink in the cabinet. There were my rolled-up socks scattered among the Ivory soap, rolls of toilet paper, and a bottle of Mr. Clean. I grabbed a pair of socks and ran back to my room to put them on.

By now I figured that Grandpa's dirty tricks weren't over yet. I was right. All of my flannel shirts hanging on hangers in my closet were still hanging there, but they had been turned inside out. I grabbed one and fixed it and put it on. Naturally, I buttoned it wrong and had to re-button it. My jeans hanging on a hook by a belt loop were inside out too. I fixed them and put them on, then saw that my belt was missing. The heck with it, I thought. I was too late to worry about a little thing like a belt.

That's when I discovered that there were no laces in my sneakers.

I stood there, staring down, my mouth hanging open like the sneakers were hanging open. I heard my mom calling up from the bottom of the stairs. "Peter! You're late, sweetie!"

Inside one sneaker was a note. "Laces on kitchen countertop."

I stuck my feet into the sneakers and tried to run downstairs. I couldn't. Without laces the sneakers kept slipping around, so I had to walk like a crazy man to keep them on my feet. I came downstairs slowly. In the second floor hallway Grandpa had his head stuck out of the door of my room. He was laughing. "Hey, Pete," he called to me, "how's it going this morning?"

"It's not funny," I said.

"War is hell" is what Grandpa said back. He laughed again, which only made me madder.

I finally made it to the kitchen. I flipflopped across the floor in my loose sneakers and practically fell into my chair at the table.

"Peter," my mom said, "why did you leave your sneaker laces on the kitchen counter?"

I took a big gulp of the orange juice that was in front of my bowl of cereal.

"Did you want me to wash your shoelaces?" Mom asked. She looked really puzzled.

"No," I said. "It was a joke." I started to eat my Cheerios real fast.

Jenny was already finished with breakfast. "You're really late, Peter," she said.

"I know it, dummy!" I shouted at her.

She looked at me like I was crazy, which maybe I was a little.

"I'd better put your laces back in while you

finish your breakfast," Mom said. I slipped my
sneakers off, which wasn't hard to do, and Mom
sat down beside me and relaced them for me.

I'd had enough breakfast by this time. I was
mad and upset and not hungry anyway. I took
the sneaker Mom had relaced and put it on and
tied it. She was still working on the other one.
"Could you try to hurry?" I said to her.

The front door slammed shut, which was
Jenny leaving the house. At least *she* wasn't
going to be late to school.

"I don't understand why you left your laces
down here," Mom said. She handed me the
other sneaker and I put it on. Then I lit out,
running for the stairs, and zoomed up to my
room like a bullet.

I was ready to find out that Grandpa had
hidden my knapsack. But there it was right by
my desk. The only thing was, it was empty. My
books were missing.

Inside the knapsack was another stupid
joke. "Books inside luggage in storage room
down the hall."

I ran like crazy to the room where we stored
the luggage. Grandpa was so devilish, I wanted
to hit him on the head with a suitcase. He had
put one book in each of the pieces of luggage,

so I had to unzip every one of them to get back all my books.

I stuffed my books into the knapsack, then ran downstairs to the coat closet. I grabbed my jacket, threw it on, and dashed out the door.

It's six blocks from my house to school. I ran until I was out of breath, then walked as fast as I could. As I rounded the corner near school I could see that the schoolyard was empty. Which meant that all the classes were going upstairs to their rooms already.

I ran across the schoolyard, and just as I got to the entrance door I remembered something. I had forgotten my lunch.

I ran upstairs and got to my class just as Mr. Pangalos, my homeroom teacher, was calling the roll. I was so out of breath that when he called my name I could barely say "Here." Steve looked across at me and asked why I was so late.

"You wouldn't believe it if I told you," I said.

32

THE LAST STRATEGY CONFERENCE

We were eating lunch at our usual table in the lunchroom. Wait a minute, that's not exactly right. Billy and Steve were eating lunch. I was *begging* lunch.

I got half an apple from Steve. Billy had a liverwurst sandwich, which he said he hated, so he gave me half of it. I hated it too. We both ate the bread and left the liverwurst. Steve said he would give me half of his milk to drink. "The second half," he said. Luckily, a nice kid named Nathaniel Robbins gave me a peanut butter cookie.

I had told the boys about my terrible morning and they laughed like crazy. "Stealing your shoelaces," Steve said, "that was a masterstroke."

"It was a rotten trick," I said.

"I like how he put each book in a different

suitcase," Billy said, and he began laughing again.

"Wait a minute," I said, "whose side are you on anyway?" I took a sip of the second half of Steve's milk, which was warm and hateful. One sip was enough.

We walked outside to the schoolyard and sat down on the steps in the sun.

"You're going to get your grandpa back for this," Steve said.

"Indubitably," I said, which was one of Steve's words.

"Not something simple, I hope," said Steve. "I think this calls for massive retaliation."

"It won't be something simple," I said.

"You've got to really get him this time," Billy said.

"Get him how?" I asked.

"I don't know," Billy said. "Paint his hair maybe?"

I wasn't even listening to Billy. Because I had already decided what I would do. It was something I had thought about doing before this, but it seemed too awful. But after what Grandpa had done to me, it seemed all right now.

"Look, guys," I said. "I know what I'm going

to do. It's terrible and I probably shouldn't do it. But I'm going to. And I'll tell you one other thing. If it doesn't work, I'm going to surrender."

"You can't!" Billy said.

"Oh, yes, I can," I said. "I'll learn to live in my stupid room. I won't like it, but I'll do it. Or else Grandpa will get me back in a more terrible way I don't even want to think about."

"You're chicken," Billy said.

"And you're right," I said. "I think I figured something out. War isn't such fun after all."

33

THE LAST ATTACK

The first thing I had to do was make Grandpa worry. I couldn't forget how nervous—make that terrified—I was while waiting for Grandpa to drop the other shoe. Now I'd give him back some of his own medicine.

I kept saying things to him like "How are you, Grandpa?" And he'd say fine. And then I'd say, "Just wait."

I also developed this little weird laugh: "*Heh-heh-heh.*" It sounded nutty even to me. So when I'd pass him on the stairs I'd turn around, look at him, and give him my "*heh-heh-heh.*"

I don't know if it had any effect or not. But it made me feel good.

I waited through all of that week he'd made me almost late for school. I didn't want it to be a school day when I got my revenge. I wanted to be home so I could see everything that was going to happen.

On Friday night, as I'd done once before, I set my alarm for the middle of the night. Sneaking down the dark, spooky stairs was a lot easier this time. The house was quiet, but I was even quieter.

The doorknob on the door turned in my hand. I sneaked in on tippy-toes. The thing I was stealing was in a glass of water on Grandpa's night table. I took the glass of water and backed slowly out of the room. Grandpa was sleeping calm and peacefully. Not even snoring. I closed the door and made it upstairs very easily.

I dumped the glass of water in the sink and let what was in the glass fall softly into my hand. I didn't want to hurt them. I took a whole bunch of face tissues from the box and wrapped them up nicely. They made a small, soft package.

I had already figured out my hiding spot. There's a large garment bag in the closet of one of the attic rooms. The kind that opens with a zipper down the side of it. Mom keeps some of Dad's old suits and a few of her dresses in it. I slid open the zipper and found a pocket in one of Dad's jackets, then put the package inside. Then I scooted back to my room, jumped into bed, and pulled the covers up.

Safe and sound. I'd done it. Now I'd have

to settle back and get some sleep. Because there sure was going to be a lot of excitement in the morning.

Grandpa was going to be very, very angry when he woke up. And I couldn't blame him. It's really a disgusting trick to steal somebody's false teeth.

34

WAR'S END

I couldn't believe I had slept peacefully through the rest of the night. But there was the time on my clock-radio: 8:30 in the morning. I lay back in my bed and tried to listen to the house. There were stirrings from someplace downstairs. Mom was probably up by now. Saturday was her supermarket day. She usually took Dad along to help her, and Jenny and me if we wanted to go.

She was in the kitchen now. I heard the sound of the pot cabinet under the stove slamming shut. She was probably beginning to prepare our Saturday morning breakfast of French toast or pancakes. I heard the water running in my parents' bathroom on the second floor. That meant Dad was up and washing.

Then I heard what I'd been listening for. Uneven footsteps sounded on the stairs as Grandpa came limping up to see me. I waited.

There was a knock on the door. "Come on in, Grandpa," I called out. The door opened and Grandpa was there. He had one hand covering his mouth, but his eyes looked awfully angry. He came into the room sideways, his face turned toward the window and away from me. "Ma feef air miffing," he said.

I stared at him. "What?"

"Ma feef," he said. "You ot ma feef, ont you?"

I got up out of bed. As I did that, Grandpa turned his back on me. "Ont ook at me!" he said.

It sounded like he was talking pig Latin or some kind of weird language.

"I don't understand you," I said.

"*Ma feef!*" shouted Grandpa. "Iff me ack ma feef, oo ittle mobber."

Suddenly the dawn came up in my brain. That's the way Grandpa spoke without his teeth. Amazing. And weird. "You're asking me to give your teeth back to you, right?" I said.

Grandpa nodded his head, his hand still covering his mouth.

"Well," I said, "you have to do something first."

"Om on, Fete, ma feef. I meed ma feef."

I translated that in my head. "You need your

teeth, right? Everybody needs teeth. But we're fighting a war here, remember?"

"Oh, Feter," he said, "ont be at way. Flease!"

"Nope," I said, "war is war. Surrender right now or I'll never ever give back your teeth. I mean it."

Grandpa turned his face toward me then. And there was such a sad look in his eyes, it almost made me want to cry. Without his teeth his mouth looked all pushed in and wrinkled. He looked so old and helpless.

Just seeing him standing there like that, a person I loved as much as anyone in the whole wide world, I felt about as low as a worm's bellybutton.

I can't explain what happened next. All I can do is tell what I did.

I ran down the hall to the closet where I'd hidden his teeth. Then I came back in a minute and handed them over, still wrapped so neat in those soft paper tissues. Grandpa took them and went into the bathroom, closing the door behind him. I heard the water running in the sink. Then he came out with his teeth back in his mouth, looking like my grandpa again.

We stared at each other, not saying anything.

I turned away from him and looked out the window. Across the street Mr. Taub was mowing his lawn. "The war is over," I said. "I hope you'll forgive me for what I did. And if it makes you feel any better, I'm so ashamed of myself, I could curl up in a ball and just disappear."

"Oh, Peter," Grandpa said, sighing.

"Maybe this is how wars get started and just go on and on," I said. "Your enemy does something bad to you, so you do something worse to him. Then he gets you back and you get him back and the whole thing gets bigger and bigger and meaner and meaner and in the end someone drops a bomb. Isn't that the way it happens?"

"Something like that," Grandpa said.

"Well," I said, "I'm sorry. I shouldn't have taken your teeth."

"It's my fault too," Grandpa said. "Don't take it all on yourself, Petey."

"I started it," I said.

"And I let you," said Grandpa. "I'm the grown-up here. I should have known better. But you know what? I enjoyed it. It was kinda fun. And I think I needed something to get over my sadness."

Grandpa came up behind me as I looked out the window. I felt his big hands on my shoulders, then his arms grabbed me and hugged me to his chest. "All of us got off on the wrong foot," he said. "Your parents took your room away and shut you up, Pete. That was mistake number one. Just because you shut someone up, it doesn't mean his hurt has gone away. There should have been a family conference, or something like that including me, and we could have figured out where I was to stay. That causes a lot of wars, too, Pete—not talking."

"I'll get used to living up here," I said.

"I'm real sorry I took your room away," Grandpa said.

"But I'm not sorry you came to live with us," I said.

Grandpa hugged me a little tight at that and kissed the top of my head. "You're a real sweet kid," he said, "but a hard guy to fight a war against."

"I still lost," I said.

"Yes," said Grandpa, "but only by the skin of my teeth."

35

BOTTOMS UP

After breakfast that day Mom, Dad, and Jenny went off to the supermarket. I chose to stay home with Grandpa. He was sitting in the kitchen, having his third cup of coffee. He looked like he was thinking hard. "You know," he said, "there has got to be another way for me to live here without taking your room away. Let's think on it, Petey."

"There's only so many rooms," I said.

"Right."

"I mean, you couldn't exactly live in the kitchen. Or in the dining room."

"Bunking in the living room is out," Grandpa said with a grin.

"Right. And the top floor is out because of your leg. Two flights up is too much."

"And the porch would be cold in winter," Grandpa said.

"That's silly," I said.

"Of course," he said. "Besides, the paper boy and the milkman would keep waking me up every morning."

"Grandpa, be serious." I laughed.

He ran a hand from the top of his face to the bottom and wiped off his smile. "Okay, serious. What's left in this old house?"

"The basement," I said. "But Dad's office is down there."

"Say, that's right," Grandpa said. "I'd kind of forgotten that. He fixed the basement up himself, didn't he? After Grandma and me had moved to Florida."

"It's kind of dingy," I said.

"Let's take a look."

I opened the door to the basement, which was in the hall right off the kitchen, and Grandpa followed me down the stairs. I put on the lights. "It's dark down here," I told Grandpa, "because only one of the three ceiling lights works."

Grandpa looked around the big room, peeking into the tiny bathroom.

"Not too promising, is it?" he said.

"Dad's not a good fixer-upper," I said.

"That's why he's an accountant," Grandpa said. He took the stepladder Dad kept against the wall and set it up, then climbed up and poked away a ceiling panel to peek through the hole. "These light fixtures weren't wired too good," he said. "But the cable is fine."

He climbed carefully down the ladder. "Do me a favor, Pete," he said. "Run on out to the garage and get me my big tape measure from out of my toolbox, would you, please? I see I got scrap paper and pencil right there on your dad's desk."

When I brought the tape measure back to him, Grandpa was talking to himself. "Heating ducts and plumbing are okay, and electricity can be pulled through. It's a start anyway."

Grandpa took the tape measure and began measuring the floor. I held the end down for him while he did the unrolling. All the time he was writing measurements on his scrap paper. Then he sat down at Dad's desk and made a sketch of the room. When he was finished he turned the paper around so I could see it.

"I'm thinking about my own little apartment down here, Pete," he said. "I think it could be real cozy."

"It's kind of dark, isn't it?" I said.

"Well, I'd fix those lights and put in a couple of lamps."

"Some of these floor tiles are loose, Grandpa."

"I'd have some carpet put down. It'll warm up the place too."

"The walls are yucky," I said.

"Paneling them will help. Make the place neat too. And I could enlarge that little bathroom, put in a stall shower. There's a gas line over in the corner, you know. I figure I could put in a little stove and maybe hang a cabinet there. So sometimes I could cook some things on my own, or make a cup of coffee down here."

"Sounds like a lot of work," I said.

"And that door leads out to the driveway, so I'd even have my own private entrance."

"I don't know, Grandpa," I said, "it's a lot of work."

"Hey, Petey." He grinned. "I used to build whole *houses*, remember? Why, one little apartment ought to be a snap. You'll help me some, won't you?"

"You bet."

"Then it'll take no time at all. And maybe a little privacy for me and a lot more privacy for the rest of you is not a bad idea. Now all we have to do is convince your dad. It's his house, after all."

I had a very bad thought. "What if he says no, Grandpa?"

"I don't think he will, Pete."

"But what if he does? Will we have to go to war with my dad?"

Grandpa threw his head back and laughed. "That would be fun, wouldn't it? But no, Petey, no more wars. From now on this family will talk everything out in the open. Peacefully, I hope."

36

BUILDING
THE PEACE

It didn't take very long to convince Dad about turning his basement office into Grandpa's new apartment. On the other hand, it wasn't as easy as I thought either.

I know that Dad and Grandpa and Mom talked about it a lot, mostly when I wasn't around. But I managed to listen in a few times from my secret spot under the stairs. Dad was worried about how much it was going to cost. Grandpa told him that he had money saved "and if I can't spend it on my daughter's house, making a place to live the rest of my life, where can I spend it?"

Dad seemed a lot more willing after that.

But he was worried about losing his office. "You'll have your office upstairs in the guest room," Grandpa explained. "Two flights up mean nothing to you," Grandpa said, "but only one flight down means a lot to me."

Dad surrendered after that, and the work began. Grandpa got these men who used to work for him in the old days to help. They mostly worked in the evenings. Moonlighting, Grandpa called it, though they kept the lights on all the time.

And I helped a lot. Grandpa showed me how to bang in a nail, how to pull a wire through a wall, and how to watch out for electricity when you are putting up lights. "What you don't want," he told me, "is a shocking experience."

It took a little more than six weeks to finish Grandpa's basement apartment. But when it was done it looked beautiful. He had a nice brown rug on the floor, a stove to make coffee and things, a new easy chair to just sit and relax in. Mom and Dad bought Grandpa a color TV of his own so he could watch his programs downstairs when we wanted to watch something else in the living room. And Grandpa's new little bathroom was so neat. One day he even let me use his brand-new shower stall. It was great.

But the best day was when Grandpa and his friends finished moving all his furniture into the basement apartment. Because when they got everything in place, they went up to the top floor and moved all my things back into my old room.

I helped them put all my stuff back in all the right places. I wanted my room to be exactly the way it was, not one thing different. I lined up the shoeboxes holding my baseball cards in the same spot they used to be. And I rehung my Hank Aaron poster right over the middle of my dresser.

When everything was in place and Grandpa and his friends left, I lay down on my bed and thought for a while. I have to tell you I had a smile on my face I just couldn't take off. I was back where I belonged, in my room where I'd always lived. It was like I had put on my favorite pair of flannel pajamas that first cold night in the fall. My room was comfortable and it fit me. I belonged to it and it to me again.

And then I started to think about some other things too. How you shouldn't always do what your friends tell you to do. They're not living your life, you are. And you have to decide what's right or wrong.

While I was lying there, feeling the best I'd felt in a long while, I heard a loud banging noise on the outside of my door. I got up to look, when Grandpa swung the door open. He had a hammer in his hand and one more nail to put in. "It's a little present I made for you," he said.

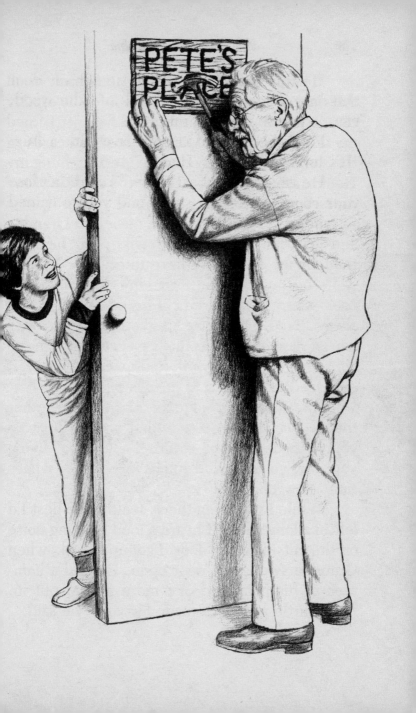

He was hanging a wooden sign on my door that had letters kind of burned into the wood. PETE'S PLACE the sign said.

I grabbed Grandpa and gave him a hug. "It's terrific," I said. "Thanks."

He gave me his best smile. "You didn't lose your room, Pete," he said, "and you've gained a grandpa."

37

FOR MY TEACHER

This last chapter is only for you, Mrs. Klein.

I want to thank you for all the encouragement you gave me when I wanted to quit so many times. And for giving me so much extra time to finish—like the whole term.

I think maybe when I grow up I might be a writer.

I got used to slipping upstairs into my dad's office to type a chapter every night after dinner. Some of the longer chapters took a week, and one of them took even longer. Mostly it was fun, but some of it was hard work. I felt so dumb, sitting there, when the words wouldn't come. But if you wait long enough and think hard enough, and your little sister keeps out of your hair, then you can do it.

I learned that starting is the hardest part. And it gets easier as you go along. But the ending is making me a little sad. I'm thinking, What will

I do tomorrow night instead of coming up here to work on my story?

Maybe I'll have to start thinking about another story.

Anyway, this is the true and real story of Peter Stokes and the war with his grandpa. I hope you like it.

And I sure hope you don't take too much off for bad spelling and grammar.